Perky Otter

Barbara deRubertis
Illustrated by Eva Vagreti Cockrille

The Kane Press
New York

Cover Design: Sheryl Kagen

Library of Congress Cataloging-in-Publication Data

DeRubertis, Barbara.
Perky Otter/Barbara deRubertis; illustrated by Eva Vagreti Cockrille.
p. cm.
"A let's read together book."—Cover.

Summary: Neighbors Perky Otter and hard-working Bert the Beaver seem to be complete opposites until Perky learns that work is not all drudgery and her neighbor learns that play can actually be fun.
ISBN 1-57565-045-2 (pbk. : alk. paper)
[1. Otters—Fiction. 2. Beavers—Fiction. 3. Work—Fiction. 4. Play—Fiction. 5. Friendship—Fiction. 6. Stories in rhyme.] I. Vagreti Cockrille, Eva, ill. II. Title.
PZ8.3.D455Pe 1998
[E]—dc21   97-44314
                                                  CIP
                                                  AC

10 9 8 7 6 5

First published in the United States of America in 1998 by The Kane Press.
Printed in Hong Kong.

LET'S READ TOGETHER is a registered trademark of The Kane Press.

www.kanepress.com

Perky Otter
loves to play.
She dips and dives.
She swims all day.

Bert the Beaver
lives next door.
He works all day—
and sometimes more.

They are two very
different neighbors.
One who plays.
And one who labors.

Neither of them
likes the other.
They make fun of
one another.

Perky says,
"That silly beaver
always works!
It's like a fever!"

Bert remarks,
"That foolish otter
never comes
out of the water.

"Sleeping late!
She'll never learn.
The *early* bird
will get the worm!"

At last, these different
neighbors meet.
It happens in the
summer heat.

Perky thinks,
"I'll have a swim."
She fills her pool
up to the brim.

She runs. She jumps.
The water swirls.
She dips and dives.
She whirls and twirls.

Then she thinks,
"Bert's on his ladder.
Work. Work. Work.
What could be sadder?

"I am such a
funny otter.
I could splash him
with some water!"

Perky runs a
faster run.
She jumps a higher
jump, for fun.

She hits the water
hard! Ker-SPLASH!
And then she hears
an awful CRASH!

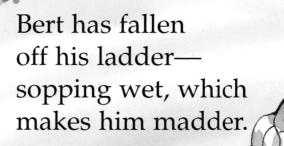

Bert has fallen
off his ladder—
sopping wet, which
makes him madder.

Perky worries,
"Are you hurt?
I'm sorry you fell
in the dirt!"

Bert is flustered.
First he sputters.
Then he mumbles
and he mutters.

"Perky, you are
such a PAIN.
You never, ever
use your BRAIN.

"But what is worse,
I've torn my shirt.
I also think
my arm is hurt."

Perky frets.
She says, "Oh, dear!
I'll get the doctor.
You stay here."

Perky Otter's
in a hurry.
Worry makes her
really scurry.

Perky races
'round the curves.
She hollers as she
swoops and swerves.

"Doctor! Doctor!
Someone's hurt!
Come and help
my neighbor Bert."

The doctor comes
and sets Bert's arm.
She says, "No work!
That could do harm."

Perky says,
"I'll be your nurse.
I'll make things better
now—not worse!

"I'll get up early.
You will see!
An 'early bird' is
what I'll be!"

23

Every morning
Perky comes
to do Bert's work.
She sings and hums.

She keeps his house
in perfect order.
Plus, she weeds
his flower border.

After lunch, Bert says,
"Please stay."
So every afternoon,
they play.

When Perky goes
back home at night,
she works some more
to put things right.

Soon Bert is better
than before.
He's learned to play!
And what is more . . .

Perky's learned
some things as well.
She thinks work's fun,
as you can tell.

Perky Otter
tells her friend,
"Together, we're
a perfect blend.

"Two parts make up
a perfect day.
First, some work . . .

and then, some play!"